D1315434

LUIGI'S ALL·NIGHT PARKING LOT

Joshua Schreier

DUTTON CHILDREN'S BOOKS
NEW YORK

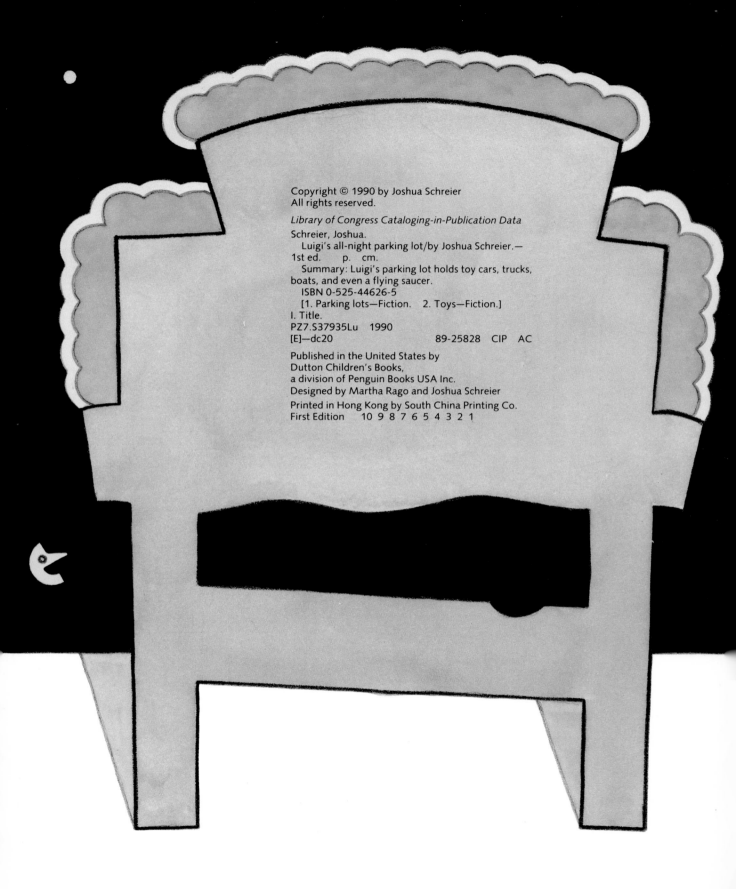

Library of Congress Cataloging-in-Publication Data
Schreier, Joshua.
  Luigi's all-night parking lot/by Joshua Schreier.—
1st ed.   p.   cm.
  Summary: Luigi's parking lot holds toy cars, trucks,
boats, and even a flying saucer.
  ISBN 0-525-44626-5
  [1. Parking lots—Fiction.   2. Toys—Fiction.]
I. Title.
PZ7.S37935Lu   1990
[E]—dc20   89-25828   CIP   AC

Published in the United States by
Dutton Children's Books,
a division of Penguin Books USA Inc.
Designed by Martha Rago and Joshua Schreier
Printed in Hong Kong by South China Printing Co.
First Edition   10 9 8 7 6 5 4 3 2 1

to Max

and his Mom

Welcome to Luigi's parking lot. It's open all night. We park cars—and other things. Nothing is too big or too small for Luigi's. The lot is empty now—but wait.

If it stops and goes, it's welcome at Luigi's. Even a London bus. No lines, no waiting. Just roll right in.

Hello, Oliver Fenderbender. You're a regular customer. Don't bang into the bus. There's a spot. No? Well, drive around and find a parking place you like. And behave yourself!

Brooom, vroom. Still haven't found your parking places? Then keep driving, everybody.

Come right in, Jeepster Robot. Need your batteries charged up tonight?

Beep! Beep! Look out, Oliver! BOOM! CRASH! Oh, no, not again! Oliver Fenderbender, I've told you a thousand times: Be careful.

Did I see Rosa? Hmmm. Sure, boats can park here. Row right in, Rosa.

Heads up! Here comes a helicopter. WHOOPA-WHOOPA-WHOOPA. Lots of business tonight. Keep moving, everybody.

I'm hungry. Time for a snack. Want some grapes, Oliver? I guess you're too busy with your tire. Okay. How about you, Rosa, Jeepster, Purpleguy? Say thank you.

Make room for the helicopter, Rosa. Good evening, Racer Redcar. Remember, no speeding.

Chugga-chugga-chugga-woo-WOOooo. Oh boy, it's train number 524. At Luigi's, we park anything— even if it needs three spaces.

Good evening, Graycar. Glad you could make it here tonight. Funny, nobody has found a parking space yet. Well, just keep rolling and rowing. Hey, look! Up in the sky . . .

RRRRRRRRRrrrrrrrrrmmmmmmmmm. Watch out, everyone! Here comes a flying saucer! WHEEeeeee!

Luigi! Time to clean up. It's getting late.
But, Papa, my parking lot's open all night.
No buts, Luigi. It's time for bed.
Just two more minutes, Papa . . . please?
All right, Luigi.

Finally. Everyone's just about parked. Good, because Luigi's All-Night Parking Lot is about to close. I'm tired.

Good night, Oliver. Good night, Rosa, Jeepster, Racer Redcar. Good night, Purpleguy. Good night, Graycar. Come tuck me in, Papa.

Good night, Papa.
Good night, Luigi.